EEP OIN'.

CARLING SPENT *YEARS* N THIS OTHER MENSION. HE MET OMAN... FELL IN VE... MARRIED... DON *ROSE* WAS BORN.

ALL THE WHILE HE CONTINUED HIS INTERDIMENSIONAL EXPERIMENTA- TION.

BUT IT WAS NOT LONG BEFORE HIS WORK CAME TO THE ATTENTION OF KIMORA. HE WAS INTENT ON HAVING CARLING'S TECHNOLOGY FOR HIS OWN... AND USING IT TO EXTEND HIS REIGN TO OTHER DIMENSIONS.

CARLING RESISTED, BUT KIMORA IS NOT A MAN WHO TAKES *NO* FOR AN ANSWER.

HIS WIFE KILLED BY KIMORA, HE WAS FORCED TO FLEE WITH ROSE THROUGH A RIFT BACK TO OUR OWN DIMENSION.

ONE WHICH KIMORA WAS ABLE TO *SLIP* THROUGH BEFORE IT FULLY *CLOSED.*

KIMORA WAS STUNNED BY HIS FIRST INTERDIMENSIONAL PASSAGE, AND CARLING WAS ABLE TO *ESCAPE* HIM...

... BUT KIMORA PURSUED HIM THROUGH THE YEARS, DETERMINED TO ACQUIRE THE TECHNOLOGY TO OPEN A PASSAGE BETWEEN OUR DIMENSIONS.

EVENTUALLY, THE DOCTOR REALIZED HIS ONLY OPTION WAS TO SEEK PROTECTION... AND FOR SUCH HE TURNED TO *US.*

WHICH IS WHERE *I* CAME IN ON THE TOKYO OP?

I ASSURE YOU THAT WE HAD NO IDEA THAT THE OPERATION HAD BEEN *COMPRO- MISED.*

SO HOW EXACTLY DID KIMORA ESCAPE AFTER HE 'DIED'? YOU TELLIN' ME HE JUST PICKED UP HIS *HEAD* AN' STROLLED OUT?

WE ARE UNSURE... AFTER HE DISAPPEARED, WE DISCOVERED... A *PINHOLE,* IF YOU WILL -- A RIFT SO SMALL THAT IT WAS VIRTUALLY UNDETECTABLE.

HE HAS BEEN ABLE TO MOVE THROUGH THIS PORT -- ALTHOUGH IT IS TOO *SMALL* AND *UNSTABLE* TO ALLOW LARGE-SCALE TRAVELING.

FOR *THAT,* HE STILL NEEDS CARLING.

ERY MUCH ELSEWHERE.

SPEAK TO ME, *ORACLE!*

THIS IS THE PLACE TO WHICH LOGAN AND CHANG JOURNEY.

HERE, *KIMORA* HAS RULED FOR MANY LIFETIMES.

TELL ME OF THAT WHICH HAS HAPPENED WHILE I WAS GONE... TELL ME OF THINGS YET TO *COME.*

OUR WORLD IS AS YOU LEFT IT, GREAT ONE.

EVEN IN HIS SELF-IMPOSED EXILE ON EARTH, HIS IRON-FISTED RULE HELD STEADY.

NOW THAT HE HAS RETURNED HOME...

...A WORLD WEEPS.

BUT OF THE FUTURE...

I SEE TWO OFF-WORLDERS WHO OPPOSE YOUR RULE. ONE IS A MAN WITH FIRE IN HIS VEINS...

...AND HE WOULD SEE YOU *DEAD.*

AH, *LOGAN.*

HOW FASCINATING WILL BE HIS *BAPTISM* TO THE WORLDS OF BEYOND...

...AND HOW *SAD* HE IS UNAWARE THAT HE IS ALREADY TOO LATE...

...THANKS TO *YOU,* MIND-THIEF.

HE WILL STILL FIGHT --

LOGAN?

IT LOOKS AS THOUGH YOU MAY LIVE AFTER ALL.

HOW LONG... HAVE I BEEN OUT?

YOU HAVE BEEN UNCONSCIOUS FOR ALMOST A *DAY*.

YOU SHOULDN'T BE ALIVE AT *ALL*.

I'VE SEEN BIGGER MEN THAN YOU FALL DEAD AFTER JUST *TOUCHING* ONE OF HER SHADOW BLADES.

THEY'RE ALL COATED WITH A LETHAL POISON.

YOU TOOK A BLADE IN THE CHEST... UP TO THE *HILT*.

LIKE I SAID... YOU SHOULD BE *DEAD*.

SHE WANTED TO PUT YOU OUT OF YOUR MISERY... CONTINUE THE MISSION *WITHOUT* YOU.

SWEET KID.

SORRY IF I DISAPPOINTED YOU, BUT... WELL, WHAT CAN I SAY?

I'VE ALWAYS BEEN A *QUICK HEALER*.

COME ON. GETTING IN ISN'T GOING TO BE AS HARD AS IT LOOKS. ACT AS IF YOU *BELONG*. WE'RE MERCENARIES LOOKING TO JOIN THE ARMY. IF ANYONE QUESTIONS YOU... *KILL* THEM.

"A RIFT? BUT HOW -- ? COULD CARLING HAVE CAPITULATED SO SOON?"

"HE WILL *NEVER* GIVE IN, CHANG. THERE IS TALK OF A *MIND-REAPER* -- A BEING WHO LOOKS BEHIND MEN'S EYES -- WHO SERVES KIMORA.

"THE WHISPERS MUST BE *TRUE*."

OFF-WORLDERS!

NO. I'LL 'ANDLE IT MY OWN WAY.

... *I* AM NOT!

KRAK

OU SPEAK *ILL* OF THE HIGH LORD KIMORA, MONK?

THESE COWARDS MAY BE WILLING TO STAND BY AND LISTEN TO YOUR *BLASPHEMY*, BUT...

LET *ANY* WHO BELIEVE IN THE MONK'S WORDS STAND BEFORE ME...

...AND I WILL STRIKE THEM DOWN IN THE NAME OF KIMORA.

OTHERWISE, STAND *ASIDE.* FOR I WILL TAKE THIS *THING* TO THE VERY GATES OF THE KIMORA'S BLESSED TOWER. HIS IMPIETY WILL BE DEALT WITH BY THE LORD *HIMSELF.*

STAND FAST, TRAVELER. NONE MAY ENTER THE INNER PALACE WITHOUT A *PASS.*

BUT... I *HAVE* A PASS.

LET ME SEE IT.

COME... CLOSER... BOTH OF YOU.

FEEL MY HAN PASS THR YOUR MINI BRAIN AND...

...SLEEP!

WELL? ARE YOU COMING?

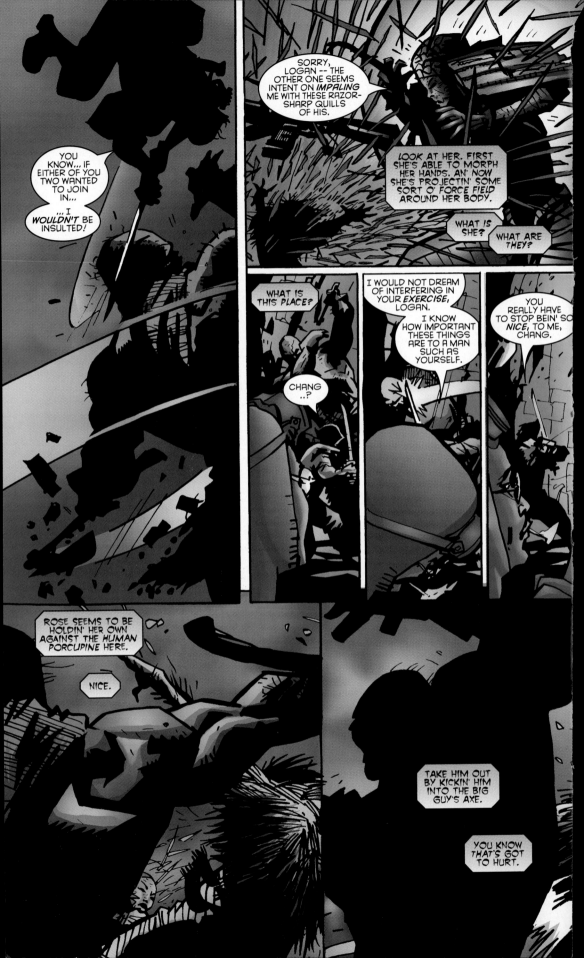